A CAPTURED
SANTA CLAUS

BY

THOMAS NELSON PAGE

WITH ILLUSTRATIONS BY
W. L. JACOBS

A CAPTURED SANTA CLAUS

I

CHRISTMAS AT HOLLY HILL

Holly Hill was a place for Christmas! Holly Hill, the old rambling Stratford homestead in Virginia, on its high hill, looking down the long slope and across the wide fields to the far woods rimming the sky. From Bob, the veteran, within a month of his teens, down to brown-eyed Evelyn, with her golden hair floating all around her, when Christmas came everyone hung up a stocking, and the visit of Santa Claus was the event of the year.

They went to sleep the night before Christmas—or rather they went to bed, for sleep was long far from their bright eyes—with delightful expectations and thrills along their backs, and with little squeakings and gurglings, like so many little white mice, and if Santa Claus had not always been so very prompt in disappearing up the chimney before daybreak he must certainly have been caught. For by the time the chickens were crowing in the morning there would be an answering twitter through the house, and with a patter of little feet and subdued laughter small, white-clad figures would steal through the dim light of dusky rooms and cold passages, opening doors with sudden bursts, and shouting "Christmas gift!" into darkened chambers, at still sleeping elders. Then they would scurry away in the gray light to rake open the hickory embers and revel in the exploration of their bulging, overcrowded stockings. Not Columbus was to be envied when those discoveries were being made. What was a new world to those treasures! The thrill of the new jack-knife remains after forty years—it had four blades, each worth a province. Envy Columbus? Perish the thought!

Such was Christmas morning at Holly Hill in the old times before the war —those times of Memory and Romance.

Thus it was that at Christmas, 1863, when the blockading lines were drawn close and there were no new toys to be had for love or money, there were much disappointment and some murmurs at Holly Hill. The children had never really felt the war until then, though their father, Major Stafford, had been off, first with his company and then with his regiment, since April, 1861. War was on the whole a pleasant experience to the boys—so many strangers came by. Battles were so interesting, and there was a bare chance of their seeing one, in which Bob was to lead a charge and capture the commanding General.

But when Christmas came and there were no presents, no "real" presents, war was realized. It was a terrible thing. From Mrs. Stafford down to little tot Evelyn there was an absence of the merriment which Christmas always brought with it. The children's mother had done all she could to collect such presents as were within her reach, but the youngsters were much too sharp not to know that the presents were "just fixed up"; and when they were all gathered around the fire in their mother's chamber that Christmas morning, looking over their presents, their little faces wore an expression of pathetic disappointment.

"I don't think much of *this* Christmas," announced freckled Ran, with characteristic gravity, looking down on his poor presents with an air of contempt. "A hatchet, a lot of old nails, and a hare-trap aren't much."

Mrs. Stafford smiled, but the smile soon died away into an expression of sadness.

"I too have to do without my Christmas gift," she said. "Your father wrote me that he hoped to spend Christmas with us, and he has not come. He has been ordered over to the Potomac."

"Never mind; he may come yet," said Bob encouragingly. "He always does what he says he's going to do." (Bob always was encouraging. That was why he was "Old Bob.") "An axe was just the thing I wanted, mamma," said he, shouldering his new possession proudly and striking the attitude of a woodman striding off. "Now I can make an abatis."

Mrs. Stafford's face lit up again. He was a sturdy boy, with wide-open eyes and a good mouth.

"And a hatchet was what I wanted," admitted Ran, affected by the example. "Besides, there are a lot of nails—now I can make my own hare-traps."

"An' I like a broked knife," asserted Charlie, stoutly, falling valiantly into the general movement, while Evelyn pushed her long hair out of her eyes, and hugged her patched-up baby, declaring:

"I love my dolly, and I love Santa Tlaus, an' I love my papa," at which her mother took the little midget to her bosom, broken doll and all, and hid her face in her tangled curls.

II

MAJOR STAFFORD COMES HOME

The end of that Christmas was better than the beginning. Major Stafford justified Bob's confidence. The holiday was not quite over when one evening Major Stafford galloped up to the gate through the mist, his black horse, Ajax, splashed with mud to his ear-tips. He had ridden him seventy miles that day to keep that tryst. The Major soon heard all about the little ones' disappointment at not receiving any new presents.

"Santa Tlaus didn' tum this Trismas, but he's tummin' *next* Trismas," said Evelyn, looking wisely up at him, that evening, from the rug, where she was vainly trying to make her doll's head stick on her broken shoulders.

"And why did he not come this Christmas, Miss Wisdom?" laughed her father, touching her caressingly with the toe of his boot.

"Tause the Yankees wouldn't let him," said she, gravely, holding her doll up and looking at it pensively, her head on one side.

"And why, then, should he come next year?"

"Taus God's goin' to make him." She turned the mutilated baby around and examined it gravely, with her shining head still set on the other side.

"There's faith for you," said Mrs. Stafford.

Her husband asked the child:

"How do you know this?"

"Tause God told me," answered Evelyn, still busy with her inspection.

"He did? When?"

"'Tother night when I saw him."

"You saw him!"

"Um—hm"—nodding her head cheerfully.

"Well! I knew she was an angel," said Major Stafford in an aside to his wife; "but—What did He say Santa Claus is going to bring you?" he asked.

The little mite sprang to her feet. "He's goin' to bring me—a—great—big —dolly—with real, sure-'nough hair, and blue eyes that will go to sleep, and her name's Miss Please-Ma'am." Her face was aglow, and she stretched her plump hands wide apart to give the size.

"She has dreamt it," said the Major in an undertone to her mother. "There is not such a doll as that in the Southern Confederacy."

The child caught his meaning. "Yes, He *is*," she insisted, "'cause I asked Him an' He said he would; and Charlie——"

Just then that youngster burst into the room, a small whirlwind in petticoats. As soon as his cyclonic tendencies could be curbed his father asked him:

"Well, what did you ask Santa Claus for, young man?"

"For a pair of breeches and a sword," answered the boy promptly, striking an attitude. "And I'm going to have 'em. I told Him I just had to have 'em."

"Well, upon my word!" laughed his father, eyeing the erect little figure and the steady, clear eyes which looked proudly up at him. "I had no idea what a young Achilles we had here. You shall have them."

The boy nodded gravely. "All right. When I get to be a man I won't let anybody make my mamma cry." He advanced a step, with head up, the very picture of spirit.

"Ah! you won't?" said his father, with a gesture to prevent his wife interrupting.

"Nor my little sister," said the young warrior, patronizingly, swelling with infantile importance.

"No; he won't let anybody make *me* ky," chimed in Evelyn, promptly accepting the proffered protection. "And he won't make me ky himself."

"But you mus'n't be a cry-baby," demanded Charlie.

"On my word, Ellen, the fellow has some of the old blood in him," said Major Stafford, laughing, much pleased. "Come here, my young knight." He drew the boy up to him and stood him before him. "I had rather have heard you say that than have won a brigadier's wreath. You shall have your breeches and your sword next Christmas if I live. Were I the king I should give you your spurs. Remember, never let any one make your mother or sister cry."

Charlie nodded in token of his acceptance of the condition.

"All right. But she mus'n't be a crybaby," he added with a glance down at Evelyn.

III

MAJOR STAFFORD GETS THE CHRISTMAS PRESENTS

When Major Stafford galloped away next day, on his return to his command, the little group at the lawn-gate shouted many messages after him. The last thing he heard was Charlie's treble, as he seated himself on the gate-post, calling to him not to forget to make Santa Claus bring him a pair of uniform breeches and a sword; and Evelyn's little voice came to him long after he could distinguish the words but he knew she was reminding him of her "dolly that can go to sleep."

Many times during the ensuing year, amid the hardships of the campaign, the privations and the fatigues of the march, and the dangers of battle, the Major heard those little voices calling to him.

In the autumn he won the three stars of a Colonel for gallantry in leading a desperate charge on a town in the heart of the enemy's land. A perilous raid had been made deep into the country. An overwhelming force had been met which defeated the object of the raid, and threatened the destruction of the entire force. The day was saved by Major Stafford. But none knew, when he dashed into the town at the head of his regiment, under a hail of bullets, that his mind was full of toyshops and clothing-stores, and that when he was so stoutly holding his position he was guarding a little boy's suit, a small sword with a gilded scabbard, and a large doll with flowing ringlets and blue eyes that could "go to sleep."

Some of his friends during that year charged the Major with growing miserly, and rallied him upon hoarding up his pay and carrying large rolls of Confederate money about his person; and when, just before the raid, he invested his entire year's pay in four or five ten-dollar gold-pieces, they vowed he was mad.

"I shall report him as a hopeless case," said Dr. Graham, the Surgeon. "A man might have reason to do this in time of peace; but when a man hoards money on his person and then exposes himself as the Major does every time we have a battle, it's proof of insanity."

The Major, however, always met these charges with a smile.

"Doctors are like other men," he said. "They think whatever they cannot understand, madness." And as soon as his position was assured in the captured town he proved his sanity.

The fight had been a sharp one, and the town had only been seized after a desperate charge. The shopkeepers had put up their shutters and were barricaded within their houses, while bullets were hailing and light field-pieces were cracking. At length it grew quiet.

The owner of a handsome store on the principal street, over which was a large sign, "Men's and Boys' Clothes," peeping out, saw a Confederate major ride up to the door, which had been hastily fastened when the fight began, and rap on it with the handle of his sword. There was something in the rap that was imperative, and the owner hastily opened the door. The officer entered.

"Good evening." He looked all about him. "Ah!" He picked up a little uniform suit of blue cloth with brass buttons.

"You have no gray ones?" he asked with a smile.

"No, sir. No use for 'em."

"What is the price of this?"

"Ten dollars," stammered the shopkeeper. "But you can have it for nothing if you will keep your men from troubling me."

To his astonishment, the Confederate officer put his hand in his pocket and laid a ten-dollar gold piece on the counter.

"Now show me where there is a toy-shop."

There was one only a few doors off, and the shopkeeper was most eager to show it. But the officer said he could find it. He went out.

The Major found and selected a boy's sword handsomely ornamented, and the most beautiful doll, over whose eyes stole the whitest of roseleaf eyelids, and which could talk as dolls talk, and do other wonderful things. He astonished this shopkeeper also by laying down another gold-piece. This left him but two or three more of the proceeds of his year's pay, and these he soon handed over a counter to a jeweller, who gave him a small package in exchange. He smiled and chatted so pleasantly with the men that when he left the shopkeepers all had new ideas of at least one "Rebel" officer.

All during the remainder of the campaign Colonel Stafford carried a package carefully sealed and strapped on behind his saddle. His care of it and his secrecy about it were the subjects of many jests among his friends in the brigade, and when in an engagement his horse was shot, and the Colonel, under a hot fire, stopped and calmly unbuckled his bundle, and during the rest of the fight carried it in his hand, there was a clamor afterward that he should disclose the contents. Even an offer to sing them a song would not appease his friends, though the Colonel had the best voice in the brigade. They must know his secret.

The brigade officers were gathered around a camp-fire that night on the edge of the bloody field. A Federal officer, Colonel Denby, who had been slightly wounded and captured in the fight, and who now sat somewhat grim and moody before the fire, was their guest.

"Now, Stafford, open the bundle and let us into the secret," they all said. "Some of us may get shot before we know it."

The Colonel, without a word, but with softened eyes, rose and, going to his saddle, which lay on the ground near by, brought the parcel to the fire. Kneeling down, he took out his knife and carefully opened the outer cover of oil-skin. Many a jest was levelled at him across the blazing logs as he did so. But a smile was on his face, and the Federal colonel thought to himself what a fine, high-bred face it was.

One said the Colonel had turned pedler, and was trying to eke out a living by running the blockade on Lilliputian principles; another wagered that he had it full of Confederate bills; a third, that it was a talisman against bullets, and so on. Within the outer covering were several others; but at length the last was reached. As the Colonel ripped carefully, the group gathered around and bent breathlessly over him, the light from the blazing camp-fire shining ruddily on their eager, weather-tanned faces. When the Colonel put in his hand and drew out a toy sword, there was a general exclamation. But when he took the doll from her soft wrapping, and then unrolled and held up a tiny jacket and a pair of little trousers not much larger than a man's hand, and just the size for a five-year-old boy, there was a dead silence and the men turned away their faces from the fire, and more than one who had boys of his own at home put his hand up to his eyes.

The Major's Christmas presents.

The Major's Christmas presents.

One of them, the bronzed and weather-beaten officer who had charged the Colonel with being a miser and who wore crepe on his sleeve, stretched himself out on the ground, flat on his face, and sobbed. As Colonel Stafford gently told his story of Charlie and Evelyn, even the grave face of Colonel

Denby looked somewhat changed in the light of the fire, and he reached over for the doll.

"May I see it?"

"Certainly." A half dozen hands were stretched out to pass it to him. He handled it tenderly.

"I, too, have a little one at home," he said in a low voice, as he handed the doll back to Colonel Stafford. "The child of my only son. He was killed at Genies's Mill."

That night Colonel Stafford and Colonel Denby slept under the same blanket.

IV

THE BOYS LEARN SOMETHING OF WAR

During the whole year the children had been looking forward to the coming of Christmas. Charlie's outbursts of petulance and not rare fits of anger were invariably checked if any mention was made of his father's injunction to take care of his mother and little sister; and at length he became accustomed to curbing himself by the recollection of the charge he had received.

If he fell and hurt himself, even badly, in his constant attempts to climb up impossible places, he would simply snap his eyes and rub himself, and presently, say, proudly, "I don't cry now; I am a knight, and next Christmas I am going to be a man, 'cause my papa's goin' to tell Santa Claus to bring me a pair of breeches and a sword." Evelyn could not help crying when she was hurt, for she was only a very little girl; but she added to her prayer of "God bless and keep my papa, and bring him safe home," the petition, "Please, God, bless and keep Santa Tlaus, and let him come here Trismas."

Old Bob and Ran, too, as well as the younger ones, looked forward eagerly to Christmas. But this year brought the war much closer to Holly Hill. Heretofore it had been to the children, even to Bob, something dim and distant, like a cloud on the horizon, with grumblings of thunder and sheet-lightning that threatened but did not strike. But now it swept up to Holly Hill like a storm, then like a flood rolled over it. The main armies passed along the great road some way off, the Northern troops pushing on and on, nearer and nearer, until the big guns could be heard to the northward, making the ground tremble and the windows shake. At such times, Mrs. Stafford would stop and listen with white face and moving lips, and the older boys would stand beside her and count the reports in low tones, for they knew a great battle was being fought, and their father might be there. What would happen in case their side was beaten and had to fall back, they trembled to think. All the horses would be taken and the corn. That would mean starvation. And, perhaps, the house might be burnt. They had heard of such things elsewhere. And they might have to "refugee." This had its pleasant side for the boys, for they would have to travel south and, maybe, camp like gypsies or the "young marooners." Bob was full of excitement as to this, and used to thrill Ran, telling how they would live, and how they would mount guard at night, and evade their pursuers—or sometimes make a stand against them, on a hill, or at a stream, throwing up their breastworks and holding them back with his gun while their mother and "the children" escaped.

Then they would go out to the stable and, seated on a manger, talk it all over with Uncle Saunders, the carriage-driver, who was guide, philosopher, and friend to them. Uncle Saunders would sometimes be consoling and sometimes almost disappointing.

"They wer'n't goin' refugeein' like a parcel of gypsies." (Uncle Saunders' ideas of camping-out were not orthodox.) "But 'tain't no danger: no Yankees could git to them. If they could, they'd 'a' been long ago," reasoned Uncle Saunders. And if a few of "them pesky raiders slipt through and got there, he'd like to see 'em git his horses—he jist would. He knew a place he could hide 'em where they'd never find 'em. Gab'rull could hardly find 'em when he comes to blow his horn."

This, at least, was exciting, and Bob was all ears. He seized the old driver by the arm.

"Where is it, Uncle Saunders? You'll tell *me*? Please. I won't tell a soul—not even Ran. You know I won't if I promise."

But no; Uncle Saunders shut up like a clam—as tight as the high-barn door.

"Well, if I guess, will you tell me? Give me three guesses: all right? Is it the thick pines the other side of the creek where the old mine used to be?"

Uncle Saunders shook his head.

"Well, is it the big marsh with the high willows, and the old wagon-track?"

"You know, boy, I ain't goin' to teck my horses—my Black George and Blifil into dat mash!"

"Well—? (strung out very long). Is it—? Let me see—I've got only one more guess—haven't I?"

"I ain't give you nothin'," said Uncle Saunders, disappointingly. "You jist guessin' around heah."

But Bob insisted that by letting him guess twice he had agreed to the plan; and, in fact, it did look so.

"Well, go on, den," said Uncle Saunders at last.

Bob, after long thought, began again, guilefully watching Uncle Saunders' oracular face to read his success or failure by his expression. "Well—is it? No, it isn't that. Is it—the deep—? No; I don't want to ask that, I know it is not that—Is it the great woods?" (This with a jump.)

Old Saunders started to shake his head, and then looked around so guilefully to see that nobody was in ear-shot, that Bob dropped his voice to its most mysterious tone as he whispered, "Is that it?"

It may be doubted whether Uncle Saunders, for all his apparent confiding of his secret to Bob, was not playing a game with him, and merely letting him suppose he had guessed his secret refuge. But, however this was, and however clever he was at acting, Uncle Saunders was not clever enough to foretell the future. One morning, as Uncle Saunders was on his way to the stable, a party of men came galloping up the hill from toward the river, and in ten minutes all Uncle Saunders' plans were overthrown, and his horses, his cherished friends, were being led away amid his reproaches and the lamentations of the boys.

"Sam, you'll have to get up earlier in the morning than this to get ahead of us," laughed one of the men.

"Dat ain't my name," said Uncle Saunders, curtly.

"You think so much of your horses, you'd better come along and attend to them. We'll pay you wages and set you free." Uncle Saunders shook his head.

"Nor, I'm goin' to stay right heah and teck keer o' my mistis and de chillern.—My master told me to teck keer ov 'em while he was away, and I'm goin' to stay heah till he comes back."

"You'll stay here till the war's over, then," said the blue-coat. "Your master, as you call him, will not be back here till then. We are going on to Richmond."

"You won't get there," said Bob with spirit. "You've been trying to get there for over three years and haven't done it."

"No, little Johnny, we haven't yet, but we're still on the way," said the soldier.

By breakfast-time the plantation had been completely overrun; and all that day the blue-clad troops were passing by.

It began to look after a little as if Bob's prediction were going to come true. The Union Armies did not reach Richmond. Their advance was stayed a few miles beyond Holly Hill. But Holly Hill and its family were well within the Federal lines, and there was no chance of being reached by any message or thing from the other side of the line. The roads, knee-deep in mud, were filled with troops in blue uniforms marching up and down, or with wagons passing backward and forward, piled high with boxes or forage. The children grew so used to them that they would go down to the roadside and watch them as they passed. The only Confederates the children ever saw now were the dejected prisoners who were being passed back on their way to prison. The only news they ever received was the rumors which reached them from Federal sources. Mrs. Stafford's heart was heavy within her, and when a day or two before Christmas she heard Charlie and Evelyn, as they sat before the fire, gravely talking of the long-expected presents which their father had promised that Santa Claus should bring them, she could stand it no longer. She took Bob and Ran into her room, and there told them that, now as it was impossible for their father to come, they must help her entertain "the children" and console them for their disappointment. The two boys responded heartily, as true boys always will when thrown on their manliness.

"I knew he could not get here," said Ran.

"I knew no one else could; but papa," said Bob, "but I hoped he might. He can do so many things no one else can do."

Mrs. Stafford shook her head.

For the next two days Mrs. Stafford and both the boys were busy. Mrs. Stafford, when Charlie was not present, gave her time to cutting out and making a little gray uniform-suit from an old coat her husband had worn when he first entered the army; while the boys employed themselves, Bob in making a pretty little sword and scabbard out of an old piece of gutter, and Ran, who had a wonderful turn for carving, in carving a doll from a piece of hard-seasoned wood.

The day before Christmas the boys lost a little time in following and pitying a small lot of prisoners who passed along the road by the gate. They were always pitying the prisoners and planning means to rescue them, for they had an idea that they suffered a terrible fate. Only one certain case had come to their knowledge. A young man had one day been carried by the Holly Hill gate on his way to the head-quarters of the officer in command of that portion of the lines, General Denby. He was in citizen's clothes, which were muddy and torn, and he was charged with being a spy. The guards with him looked grim. His face was white, and yet he was a fierce-looking young fellow, speaking scornfully to his guards. Bob and Ran returned to the house, full of excitement, and spent some time that night planning how they might rescue him. Their plan included no less than the capture of General Denby himself. Bob mapped it all out—how he would cross the creek, dodging the picket at the bridge, slip past the sentries, and walking into the farm-house where the General had his headquarters, would seize him and force him to write a release of the prisoner.

The next morning, Ran, who had risen early to visit his hare-traps, rushed into his mother's room, white-faced and wide-eyed. "Oh! mamma!" he gasped, "they have hung him, just because he had on those clothes. Uncle Saunders heard all about it."

Mrs. Stafford, though she was much moved herself, endeavored to explain to the boy that this was one of the laws of war, but Ran's mind was not able to comprehend the principles which imposed so cruel a sentence for what he deemed so harmless a fault.

"It's that old General Denby!" he exclaimed, hotly. "Even his own soldiers say he works them to death. I wish somebody would capture him."

This act and some other measures of severity gave General Denby a reputation for much harshness among the few old residents who yet remained at their homes within the lines, and the boys used to gaze at him furtively as he would ride by, grim and stern, followed by his staff. Yet there were those who said that General Denby's rigor was simply the result of a high standard of duty, and that at bottom he had a soft heart.

The children, however, could never bear to think of him, and when he would pass along with his staff, as he sometimes did, while they were watching beside the road, and would look at them with something very like a smile in his eyes, they would turn their heads away for fear he would speak to them.

V

THE SPY

The approach of Christmas was marked even in the Federal camps, and many a song and ringing laugh were heard around the camp-fires glowing along the hills and in the tents and little cabins used as winter-quarters, over the boxes which were pouring in from home.

The troops in the camps near General Denby's head-quarters on Christmas Eve had been larking and frolicking all day like so many boys, preparing for the festivities of the evening, when they proposed to have a great entertainment; and the General, as he sat in the smoky front room in the old farm-house used as his head-quarters, writing official papers, had more than once during the afternoon half-frowned at the noise and shouting outside. It disturbed him. A holiday occasion was not the easiest time for a general in command, especially when the enemy lay in force scarcely five miles away. The men were apt to think that at such a time discipline should be relaxed, and they be allowed to take it easy. And such an occasion was just the moment when his opponent, a general as watchful as he was able, was likely to make an attack. News had reached him through his scouts that such an attack was probable. Moreover, the General had been working all day answering despatches from men in Washington, telling him to do things that were either impossible or had been done long ago. And, to crown it all, the chimney smoked badly.

At length, however, late in the afternoon, he finished his work, and having dismissed his Adjutant, he locked the door, and pushing aside all his business papers, took from his pocket a little letter and began to read.

As he read, the stern lines of the grim soldier's face relaxed, and more than once a smile stole into his eyes and stirred the corners of his grizzled mustache.

The letter was scrawled in a large, childish hand, and many of the words were interlined. It ran:

"MY DEAREST GRANDPAPA: I want to see you very much. I send you a Christmas gift. I made it all myself. I hope to get a whole lot of dolls and other presents. I love you. I send you all these kisses ************. You must kiss them every one. Don't I write well?

"Your loving little granddaughter,
"LILY."

When he had finished reading, the old veteran gravely lifted the letter to his lips and pressed a kiss on each of the little spaces, so carefully drawn by the childish hand.

This done, he took out his handkerchief and blew his nose violently as he walked up and down the room. He even muttered something about "the fire smoking." Then he sat down once more at his table, and, placing the little letter before him, began to write. As he wrote, the fire smoked more than ever, and the sounds of revelry outside reached him in a perfect uproar; but he no longer frowned, and when the strains of "Dixie" came in faintly at the window, sung in a clear, rich, mellow solo, though for a moment he looked surprised, he sat back in his chair and listened.

> "I wish I were in Dixie, away, away;
> In Dixie's land I'll take my stand,
> To live and die for Dixie land,
> Away, away, away down South in Dixie!"

sang the voice, full and sonorous.

When the song ended, there was an outburst of applause, and shouts apparently demanding some other song, which was refused, for the noise grew to a tumult. The General rose and walked to the window. A large crowd had gathered about a campfire not far from his window, and in the midst, lifted up on a box, and clearly outlined against the firelight stood the singer, a tall, straight man with a long beard and civilian's clothes. Suddenly the uproar hushed, for the voice began again. But this time it was a hymn:

> "While shepherds watched their flocks by night,
>   All seated on the ground,
> The Angel of the Lord came down,
>   And glory shone around."

Verse after verse was sung, the men pouring out of their tents and huts to listen to the music.

> "All glory be to God on high,
>   And to the earth be peace;
> Good will henceforth from Heaven to men
>   Begin and never cease!"

"Begin and never cease," sang the singer to the end.

When the strain died away, there was dead silence for a little space, and then the talk began on a lower key.

The General stood for a moment, then turned from the window, finished his letter and sealed it. Carefully folding up the little sheet which lay before him, he replaced it in his pocket, and, going to the door, summoned the orderly who was just without.

"Mail that at once," he said.

"Yes, sir." The soldier saluted and turned to leave.

"By the way, who was that singing out there just now?—I mean that last one, who sang 'Dixie' and the hymn?"

"Only a pedler, sir, I believe."

The General's eyes fixed themselves on the soldier.

"Where did he come from?"

"I don't know, sir. Some of the boys had him singing."

"Tell Major Dayle to come here immediately," said the General.

In a moment the officer summoned entered, a stout, round-faced man, who looked as if he took the world easy. He appeared somewhat embarrassed.

"Who was this pedler?" asked the commander.

"I—I don't know——" began the other.

"You don't know! Where did he come from?"

"From Colonel Watchley's camp—directly," said he, relieved to shift a part of the responsibility.

"How was he dressed?"

"In citizen's clothes."

"What did he have?"

"A pack—a few toys, and trinkets, and books."

"What was his name?"

"I did not hear it."

"And you let him go!" The General's eyes snapped.

"Yes, sir; I don't think——" he began.

"No, I know you don't," said the General. "Have I not given strict orders? He was a spy. Where has he gone?"

"I—I don't know. He cannot have gone far."

"Report yourself under arrest," said the commander, sternly.

The officer, after waiting a moment, walked off scowling. Walking to the door, the General said to the sentinel:

"Call the corporal, and tell him to request Captain Albert to come here immediately."

In a moment an alert, vigorous-looking young officer came up, and the General gave him an order.

"He must be found and not allowed to escape," he said in closing.

"Yes, sir: I'll find him," he said, as he hurried off.

Ten minutes later a small body of horsemen rode rapidly out of camp in the direction the pedler had taken. The picket at the bridge across the little stream below the camp had seen nothing of the pedler, and the men separated and began to visit the camps stretched along the slopes above the stream.

An hour or two later Captain Albert reported that he had traced the spy to a place just over the creek, where he was believed to be harbored. He wanted more men to surround the house.

"Take a detail and arrest him, or burn the house," ordered the General, angrily. "It is a perfect nest of treason—even the slaves are rebels!" he said to himself, as he walked up and down, as though in justification of his savage order. He put his hand in his pocket. It struck a little square envelope.

"Or wait," he called to the captain, who was just withdrawing. "I will go there myself, and take it for my head-quarters. It is a better place than this. I cannot stand this smoke any longer. That will break up their treasonable work."

VI

SANTA CLAUS PASSES THE LINES

All that day the tongues of the two little ones at Holly Hill had been chattering unceasingly of the expected visit of Santa Claus that night. Mrs. Stafford had tried to explain to Charlie and Evelyn that it would be impossible for Santa Claus to bring them their presents this year; but she was met with the undeniable and unanswerable statement that their father had promised them. Before going to bed they had hung their stockings on the mantelpiece right in front of the chimney, so that Santa Claus would be sure to see them.

The mother had broken down over Evelyn's prayer, "not to forget my papa, and not to forget my dolly," and "to take care of my papa and of Santa Claus and not to let the Yankees hurt 'em," and her tears fell silently after the little ones were asleep, as she put the finishing touches to the tiny gray uniform for Charlie. She was thinking not only of the children's disappointment, but of the absence of him on whose promise they had so securely relied. He had been away now for a year, and she had had no word of him for many weeks. Where was he? Was he dead or alive? Mrs. Stafford sank on her knees by the bedside.

"O God, give me faith like this little child!" she prayed again and again. She was startled by hearing a step on the front portico and a knock at the door.

Bob, who was working in front of the hall-fire, went to the door. His mother heard him answer doubtfully some question. She opened the door of her chamber and went out into the hall. A stranger with a large bundle or pack on his back stood on the threshold. His clothes were shabby and old, his hat, which was still on his head, was pulled down over his eyes, and he wore a beard.

"An', leddy, wud ye bay so koind as to shelter a poor sthranger for a noight at this blissed time of pace and good-will?" he said, in a strong Irish brogue.

"Certainly," said Mrs. Stafford, with her eyes fixed on him. She moved slowly up to him. Then, by an instinct, quickly lifting her hand, she pushed his hat back from his eyes. Her husband clasped her in his arms.

"My darling!"

Bob, with a cry, seized him. "I knew you'd come, father," he said.

"They all said you would," declared Mrs. Stafford.

"Well, I *had* to come. I had given my word," said Colonel Stafford, smiling.

The Colonel was borne into the hall.

A little later the pack was opened, and such a treasure-house of toys and things was displayed as surely never greeted any other eyes. The smaller children, including Ran, were not awakened, at their father's request, though Mrs. Stafford wished to wake them to see him. But Bob was let into the secrets, except that he was not permitted to see a small package which bore his name. Mrs. Stafford and the Colonel were like two children themselves as they "tipped" about, stuffing the long stockings with candy and toys. The beautiful doll with flaxen hair, all arrayed in silk and lace, was seated, last of all, securely on top of Evelyn's stocking, with her wardrobe just below her, where she would greet her young mistress when she should first open her eyes, and Charlie's little blue uniform was pinned beside the gray one his mother had made, with his sword buckled around the waist.

Bob was at last dismissed to his room, and the Colonel and Mrs. Stafford settled themselves before the fire, hand in hand, to talk over the past.

They had hardly started, when Bob rushed down the stairs and dashed into their room.

"Papa! papa! the yard is full of Yankees!"

Both the Colonel and Mrs. Stafford sprang to their feet.

"Through the back door!" cried Mrs. Stafford, seizing her husband.

"He cannot get out that way—they are everywhere—all around the house; I saw them from my window," gasped Bob, just as the sound of trampling without came to their ears.

"Oh! what will you do! Those clothes! If they catch you in those clothes!" began Mrs. Stafford, and then stopped, her face growing ashy pale. Bob also turned even whiter than he had been before. He remembered the fate of the young man who was found in citizen's clothes in the autumn. He burst out crying. "Oh, papa! will they hang you?" he sobbed.

"I hope not, my son," said the Colonel. "Certainly not if I can prevent it." A gleam of humor stole into his eyes. "It's an awkward fix, certainly," he added, gravely.

A number of footsteps sounded on the porch, and a thundering knock shook the door.

"You must conceal yourself," cried Mrs. Stafford. "Come here." She pulled him almost by main force into a closet or entry, and locked the door, just as the knocking was renewed. As the front door was apparently about to be broken down, she went out into the hall. Her face was deadly white, and her lips were moving in prayer.

"Who's there?" she called, tremblingly, trying to gain time.

"Open the door immediately, or it will be broken down," replied a stern voice.

She turned the great iron key in the heavy, old, brass lock, and a dozen men pushed into the hall. They all waited for one, a tall, elderly man in a general's fatigue-uniform, with a stern face and a grizzled beard. He addressed her.

"Madam, I have come to take possession of this house as my head-quarters."

Mrs. Stafford bowed, unable to speak. She was sensible of a feeling of relief; there was a gleam of hope. If they did not know of her husband's presence—? But the next word destroyed it.

"We have not interfered with you up to the present time, but you have been harboring a spy here, and he is here now."

"There is no spy here, and has never been," said Mrs. Stafford, with dignity. "But if there were, you should not know it from me. It is not the custom of our people to deliver up those who have sought their protection." She spoke with much spirit.

The officer removed his hat. His keen eye was fixed on her white face. "We shall search the premises," he said, still sternly, but more respectfully than he had yet spoken. "Major, have the house thoroughly searched."

The men went striding off, opening doors and looking through the rooms. The General took a turn up and down the hall. He walked up to a door.

"That is my chamber," said Mrs. Stafford, quickly.

The officer fell back. "It must be searched," he said.

"My little children are asleep in there," said Mrs. Stafford, her face quite white.

"It must be searched," repeated the General, more gently. "Either they must do it, or I. You can take your choice."

Mrs. Stafford stood aside and made a gesture of assent. She could not trust her voice. He opened the door and stepped across the threshold. There he stopped. His eye took in the scene. Charlie was lying in the little trundle-bed in the corner, calm and peaceful, and by his side was Evelyn, her little face looking like a flower, lying in the tangle of golden hair which fell over her pillow. The noise disturbed her slightly, for she smiled suddenly, and muttered something about "Santa Tlaus" and a "dolly." The officer's gaze swept the room, and fell on the overcrowded stockings hanging from the mantel. He advanced to the fireplace and examined the doll and trousers closely. With a curious expression on his face he leant over and gazed earnestly down at the two little heads on their pillow. Then he turned and walked out of the room, closing the door softly behind him.

"Major," he said to the officer in charge of the searching party, who descended the stairs just then, "take the men back to camp, except the sentinels. There is no spy here."

In a moment Mrs. Stafford came out of her chamber. The old officer was walking up and down in deep thought. Suddenly, as the last soldier disappeared through the door, he turned to her: "Mrs. Stafford, be so kind as to go and tell Colonel Stafford that General Denby desires him to surrender himself."

Mrs. Stafford was struck dumb. She was unable to move or to speak.

"Kindly present my compliments and say he need not hurry; I shall wait for him," said the General, quietly, throwing himself into an arm-chair, and looking steadily into the fire.

VII

BOB SECURES A UNIFORM

As his father concealed himself, Bob had left the chamber. He was in a perfect agony of mind. He knew that his father could not escape, and if he were found dressed in citizen's clothes he felt that he could have but one fate. Once the men went toward the passage that led through to the rear entry in which his father was concealed. Bob's heart stood still; but he acted quickly. He flung himself on the floor right in the entrance and began to work quietly by the dim firelight. The searchers passed by. All sorts of schemes for rescue entered his head. Suddenly he thought of a small group of prisoners he had seen pass by about dark. He had talked with one of them, a major. A guard said they were on their way to General Denby's camp. He would save him! Putting on his hat, he opened the front door and slipped out. A sentinel tramping up and down on the porch accosted him surlily to know where he was going.

"Won't you come in and get warm?" said Bob, hospitably.

"Can't. Wish I could. It's cold enough out here. Cold as th' State of Maine. I wish I was in old York right now by a good stove."

"I wish you were, too," said Bob, with sincerity.

"I'd give a mite to see that old white steeple again, and the moonlight on the snow stretching down toward the mill-pond; and hear the tide ripping in."

"What do you do with your prisoners when you catch them?" inquired Bob.

"Send some on to prison—and hang some."

"I mean when you first catch them."

"Oh, they stay in camp. We don't treat 'em bad, without they be spies. There's a batch at camp now, got in this evening—sort o' Christmas-gift." The soldier laughed as he stamped his feet to keep warm.

"Where's your camp?" Bob asked.

"About a mile from here, right on the road, or rather right on the hill at the edge o' the pines 'yond the crick."

The boy left him, and sauntered in and out among the other men who were building a fire in the yard. Presently he moved on to the edge of the lawn beyond them. No one took further notice of him. In a second he had slipped through the gate, and was flying across the field. He knew every foot of the ground as well as a hare, for he had been hunting and setting traps over it since he was as big as little Charlie. He had to make a detour at the creek to avoid the picket at the bridge, and the dense briers in the bottom were very bad and painful. However, he worked his way through, though his face and hands were severely scratched. Into the creek he plunged. "Outch!" He had stepped into a hole up to his waist, and the water was as cold as ice. However, he was soon through, and at the top of the hill he could see the glow of the camp-fires lighting up the sky.

He crept up cautiously, and saw the dark forms of the sentinels pacing backward and forward wrapped in their overcoats, now lit up by the fire, then growing black against its blazing embers, then lit up again, and passing away into the shadow. How could he ever get by them? His heart began to beat and his teeth to chatter, but he walked boldly up.

"Halt! who goes there?" cried the sentry, bringing his gun down and advancing on him.

Bob kept on, and the sentinel, finding that it was only a boy, looked rather sheepish. To the men about the camp-fire his appearance was the signal for fun.

"Don't let him capture you, Jim," called one of them; "Call the Corporal of the Guard," another; "Order up the reserves," a third. "He's a Christmas-gift for you; I'm going to put him in your stocking," laughed one. "It's big enough to hold him," said another.

Bob had to undergo something of an examination. Where had he come from?

"I know the little Johnny," said one of the men. "He lives over in the white house on the hill to that side of the creek."

They told Bob to draw up to the fire, and made quite a fuss over him. Bob had his wits about him and soon learned that a batch of prisoners were at a fire a hundred yards farther back. He therefore made his way over there, although he was advised to stay where he was and get dry, and had many offers of a bunk from his new friends, some of whom followed him over to where the prisoners were.

Most of the prisoners were quartered for the night in a hut before which a guard was stationed. One or two, however, sat around the camp-fire, chatting with their guards. Among these was a major in full uniform. Bob singled him out: he was just about his father's size.

Bob was instantly the centre of attraction. Again he told them he was from Holly Hill; again he was recognized by one of the men.

"Run away to join the army?" asked one.

"No," said Bob, his eyes flashing at the suggestion.

"Lost?"

"No."

"Mother whipped you?"

"No."

As soon as their curiosity had somewhat subsided, Bob, who had hardly been able to contain himself, said to the Confederate major in a low undertone:

"My father, Colonel Stafford, is at home, concealed, and the Yankees have taken possession of the house."

"Well?" said the Major, looking down at him as if casually.

"He cannot escape. He came to-night through the lines, and he has on citizen's clothes, and—" Bob's voice choked suddenly as he gazed at the Major's uniform.

"Well?" The prisoner for a second looked sharply down at the boy's earnest face. Then he put his hand under his chin, and lifting it, looked into his eyes. Bob shivered and a sob escaped him.

The Major placed his hand firmly on his knee. "Why, you are wringing wet," he said, aloud. "I wonder you are not frozen to death." He rose and stripped off his coat. "Here, get into this;" and before the boy knew it the Major had bundled him into his coat, and rolled up the sleeves so that Bob could use his hands. The action attracted the attention of the rest of the group, and several of the soldiers offered to take the boy and give him dry clothes.

"No, sir," laughed the Major; "this boy is a rebel. Do you think he will wear one of your Yankee suits? He's a little major, and I'm going to give him a major's uniform."

In a minute he had stripped off his trousers, and was helping Bob into them, standing himself in his underclothes in the icy air. The legs were twice too long for the boy, and the waist came up to his arm-pits.

"Now go home to your mother," said the Major, laughing at his appearance; "and some of you fellows get me some clothes or a blanket. I'll wear your Yankee uniform out of sheer necessity."

Bob trotted around, keeping as far away from the light of the camp-fires as possible. He soon found himself unobserved, and reaching the shadow of a line of huts, and keeping well in it, he came to the edge of the camp. He watched his opportunity, and when the sentry's back was turned he slipped out into the darkness. In an instant he was flying down the hill. The heavy clothes impeded him, and he stopped only long enough to snatch them off and roll them into a bundle, and sped on his way again. He struck the main road, and was running down it as fast as his legs could carry him, when he suddenly found himself almost on a group of dark objects who were standing in the road just in front of him. One of them moved. It was the picket. He had forgotten all about them. Bob suddenly stopped. His heart was in his throat.

Bob trotted around, keeping as far away from the light of the camp-fires as possible.

Bob trotted around, keeping as far away from the light of the camp-fires as possible.

"Who goes there?" said a stern voice. Bob's heart beat as if it would spring out of his body.

"Come in; we have you," said the man, advancing.

Bob sprang across the ditch beside the road, and putting his hand on the top rail of the low fence, flung himself over it, bundle and all, flat on the other side, just as a blaze of light burst from the picket, and the report of a carbine startled the silent night. The bullet grazed the boy's arm, and crashed through the rail. In a second Bob was on his feet. The picket was almost on him. Seizing his bundle, he dived into the thicket as a half-dozen shots were sent ringing after him, the bullets hissing and whistling over his head. Several men dashed into the woods after him in hot pursuit, and a couple more galloped up the road to intercept him; but Bob's feet were winged, and he slipped through briers and brush like a scared hare. They scratched his face and threw him down, but he was up again. Now and then a shot crashed behind him, but he did not care for that; he thought only of being caught.

A few hundred yards up the stream he plunged into the water, and wading across, was soon safe from his pursuers. Breathless, he climbed the hill, made his way through the woods, and emerged into the open fields. Across these he sped like a deer. He had almost given out. What if they should have caught his father, and he should be too late! A sob escaped him at the bare thought, and he broke again into a fast run, wiping off with his sleeve the tears that would come. The wind cut him like a knife, but he did not mind that.

As he neared the house he feared that he might be stopped again and the clothes taken from him, so he paused for a moment, and slipped them on once more, rolling up the sleeves and legs as well as he could. He crossed the yard undisturbed. He went around to the same door by which he had come out, for he thought this his best chance. The same sentinel was there, walking up and down, blowing his cold hands. Had his father been arrested? Bob's teeth chattered, but it was with suppressed excitement.

"Your clothes seem to 'a' grown a mite since you went out?" said the sentry, quizzically.

"Yes, I was co-co-cold," stammered Bob.

"'Tis pretty cold," said the sentry.

"Ye—es," gasped Bob.

"Your mother's been out here, looking for you, I guess," said the soldier, with much friendliness.

"I rec—reckon so," panted Bob, moving toward the door. Did that mean that his father was caught? He opened the door, and slipped quietly into the corridor.

General Denby still sat silent before the hall-fire. Bob listened at the chamber-door. His mother was weeping; his father stood calm and resolute before the fire. He had determined to give himself up.

"If you only did not have on those clothes!" sobbed Mrs. Stafford. "If I only had not cut up the old uniform for the children!"

"Mother! mother! I have one!" gasped Bob, bursting into the room and tearing off the unknown major's uniform.

" I'm goin' to get my papa," said the tiny swordsman.